BITS &
PIECES

© 1971 Young World Productions Ltd.
Printed by Publicaciones Reunidas, S.A. Barcelona. Spain
Dep. Leg.: B. 8 102-71
SBN 7238 07191

MAGNUS MOUSE AND
THE TREASURE CHEST

TOLD BY EDWARD HOLMES

ILLUSTRATED BY HORACE FAITHFUL

YOUNG WORLD  PRODUCTIONS

LIMITED

London

IT takes all kinds of people to make a town, and in Woodsey Newtown, the special town of the Woodsey folk, this really was true. All kinds of people lived there.

For example, you couldn't have found two more different people than Magnus Mouse, and Jasper Scallywag-Fox. Magnus was very very honest, rather timid but hard working. If Magnus started a job, you could depend on it that he would finish it. Jasper, now, was a bit of a rogue, very bold and boastful in his talk and scared to bits of anything that looked like work. If he started anything, he seldom finished it—not, at any rate, in the way he said he would.

Magnus was the Woodsey carpenter. He could make anything out of wood. Jasper was the Town Hall caretaker and he took care to do as little as possible. All the real work, like polishing the big brass door-knobs, he left to his assistant caretaker, Squeevey Squirrel.

On this particular fine spring day,
Magnus Mouse was working in the Town
Hall. He was putting up some bookshelves
in the study of the Mayor, Mr Aristotle Mole.
J. Scallywag-Fox was sitting in the Mayor's
chair, watching him do it.

"Hm!" said Jasper, looking down his long nose at Magnus. "You seem to be using very nice wood for the shelves—but where are your nails, my good man?"

"I don't use nails, Mr Fox. . ."

"No nails? Good gracious me! How do you expect the wood to hold together, if you don't use nails? I never heard of such a thing!"

"Please, Mr Fox," explained Magnus very

timidly, "I make all the wooden bits so that
they fit together properly. I don't need
nails; besides, nails split the wood, you
know."

Jasper was just about to reply to this,
when the door opened, and Mr Mole, the
Mayor, came in. Jasper hurriedly jumped up
from his chair.

"Aha!" said Mr Mole. "The shelves are
coming along nicely, I see. My word, they do

look nice. What a splendid job!"

"Just what I said, Mr Mayor!" declared Jasper. "They're made the latest way, you know. The wood is all fitted together, so that you don't have to use nails. Splits the wood, you know. You may rely on me to see that Mr Mouse here does the job properly."

"I'm sure I can," said Mr Mole dryly. He knew all about Jasper and he wasn't fooled for one moment, "but I don't think Mr Mouse will make any mistakes. Now where's my case? I only looked in to collect it . . ."

Jasper quickly found Mr Mole's case, and handed it to him before the Mayor hurried away. Jasper sat down in the Mayor's chair again and took out his big watch.

"Five minutes past one—you may stop work for lunch, my good man," said Jasper.

"Thank you, Mr Fox," said Magnus. "I've brought my sandwiches." He put down his tools and began to unpack a neat little lunch box. "Would you like a sandwich, Mr Fox?

I'm afraid they're only cheese."

"How very kind of you," replied Jasper, in gracious tones. To tell the truth, he had been hoping to share Magnus's lunch. "I am very fond of cheese. Thank you—I'll take two, while I'm about it. My—what a nice lot of cheese. How good!"

"I'm glad you like them, Mr Fox," said Magnus. "They're our special family sort— we always put the cheese on the outside, with a slice of bread in the middle. It seems to make them more tasty than they are the other way round. Us Mouses eat a lot of cheese, you know."

"Mmmmm!" mumbled Jasper through a mouthful of cheese. "How very interesting." He munched rapidly, for an idea had suddenly come to him. Jasper was always full of ideas, generally for making money without doing any work and that was the sort of idea he had got now. "Speaking of cheese, you would have liked my Uncle Stilton. Very fond of cheese, he was. I never knew anyone who ate as much cheese as he did. I doubt whether he could have afforded to buy that much cheese. But then he didn't have to—not after his great discovery."

"His great discovery?" Magnus Mouse was wide-eyed with interest, his first sandwich poised half way to his mouth. "What was his great discovery, Mr Fox?"

"That is a family secret," said Jasper,

very solemnly, "but since you are clearly a
great cheese-lover, I think I can see my way
to telling you. Of course, you must promise
never to tell anyone else."

"Oh yes—I promise!" said Magnus.

Jasper looked swiftly around to be sure
that nobody could overhear them and
lowered his voice.

"My uncle, the great Stilton Scallywag-
Fox, discovered a way of growing the most

excellent cheese from seeds!" he whispered.

"Coo!" said Magnus, his eyes round with wonder, for he believed every word that Jasper was saying. "What a wonderful discovery!"

"Yes," said Jasper, really warming up to the tale he was telling, "a wonderful discovery indeed. Well, I remember as a boy, visiting him at Urth—that was the name of his estate, you know—and being taken round the cheese garden. There they were, row upon row of beautiful cheese trees, with lovely red round cheeses growing from the branches."

"What a beautiful sight!" breathed Magnus, so carried away by Jasper's tale that he wasn't even bothering to eat his lunch. "Do the cheeses still grow in his garden, Mr Fox?"

"Alas, no," sighed Jasper, "that is all long gone, for when my Uncle Stilton died, there was nobody who knew how to look after

the trees and they withered and died." He reached over, and took the last sandwich out of Magnus's lunch box. "Thank you—I will have another sandwich, if you insist. Yes—I fear that the cheese garden is no more. It takes a very clever gardener to grow cheese trees, you know."

"I do a lot of gardening!" cried Magnus, in great excitement. "Perhaps I could grow cheese trees, if I tried!"

"Why of course!" declared Jasper, pretending to look very surprised. "You are quite famous as a gardener. I well remember your prize marrows! I am sure that if anyone can grow cheese trees, it is you. What would you need, Mr Mouse?"

"Well—I'd have to have some seeds. I think if I had just a few seeds, I could do the rest. I'm very good at growing things . . ."

"Seeds—seeds—I wonder . . ." Jasper paced up and down, pretending to think very hard. "I kept many of my uncle's old things

after the estate was sold up and there are
a lot of old tins from his potting shed."

Of course, Jasper was making all this up,
although he really had had an Uncle Stilton,
a rather gentle old chap who'd kept a sweet
shop.

"I shall search through my uncle's things
and if there are any cheese seeds there, you
shall have them!" he declared.

"Thank you very much indeed!" breathed
Magnus. "Of course, I'll pay you . . ."

"A small sum would be acceptable—but
no matter. Let us discuss that when I have
found the seeds. I will look for them tonight

and tomorrow, you shall have them!"

Well, you know how it is when "tomorrow" is rather special. It seems as if it never will come. Magnus hardly slept a wink that night, thinking of the wonderful cheese garden he was going to have. When morning came at last, he hurried round to the Town Hall to meet Jasper. He paid Jasper five pounds for a small sack of shiny seeds, and hurried home with them, absolutely wild with joy.

"I am going to grow some cheese,
smelling lovely on the breeze,
we'll have more than we can eat,
life will be so very sweet,
and whether it's Cheddar or Cam-em-bert,
I'll eat it like a real expert!"

So sang Magnus as he skipped on his way home, with the sack of seeds over one shoulder. The other Woodsey folk who saw him thought that he had gone potty!

Poor Magnus! He hadn't a hope of

growing cheeses. Those seeds were just
millet seeds, which that old rascal Scallywag
Fox had dipped in red ink.

When he got home, Magnus put the seeds
away very carefully in the special little
cupboard that was part of his sideboard,
where they kept valuable things like the set
of silver cheese knives that he and his wife
Martha had had for a wedding present.

He didn't tell even Martha what he was

doing, because he had promised Scallywag-Fox that he would keep the secret and Magnus always kept his promises.

Then Magnus went to his little tool shed, got out his best spade and started digging in a quiet corner of the garden. It wasn't that he meant to plant the seeds then and there—it was just that he always did a bit of digging when he wanted to think.

And those cheese seeds needed a very big think. So Magnus dug and thought and dug some more and thought some more . . .

Sker-rawk! His spade scraped on something very hard, just under the ground.

"Bother!" said Magnus. Whatever it was, it had interrupted his think.

Now if you're a keen gardener, like Magnus, large hard lumps of stuff in your garden are something you hate. So Magnus set to work to dig it out.

"Nasty great rock!" grumbled Magnus to himself. "Better out than in!.'

He levered at the lump with his spade and it moved—moved, and as he pushed some more, it broke upwards out of the earth.

Magnus gasped with surprise! It was a big old brass-bound chest!

"Goodness grumpkins!" said Magnus. "I do believe it's a treasure chest!"

At that moment, Bungle Bunny, who was the Woodsey postman, came up the garden path to deliver a letter.

"Goodness! That looks like a treasure chest!" said Bungle.

"Yes! Isn't it exciting!" cried Magnus. "Would you please give me a hand to pull it out?"

Bungle helped, very willingly. The chest was locked with two big padlocks and on the top were the initials "B.B."

"B.B." read Bungle Bunny, when they had pulled the chest onto level ground. "I suppose those are the initials of who it belonged to. I wonder what they stand for?"

"Bungle Bunny?" suggested Magnus.

"Why—yes—of course!" said Bungle. "I thought that they sounded familiar. But that's not my chest. I've never seen it before."

"It's a myskery—a real myskery!" breathed Magnus, who what with the cheese seeds and now this, had never had such an exciting time in his life before.

"I wonder what's inside?" said Bungle Bunny. "Those padlocks look jolly strong. I

don't suppose the key's anywhere around . . ."

Bungle peered hopefully into the hole, but there was no key to be seen.

"Perhaps we could break it open with a chopper," he suggested. "I'm dying to know what's inside. Have you got a chopper?"

Magnus looked horrified.

"Ooo! We couldn't do anything like that! This is treasure trove . . ."

"It is?"

"Oh yes. You have to tell the Proper Authorities about it and they decide whether you can keep it, or not."

"Is there a Proper-what-you-said in Woodsey?" Bungle wanted to know.

"Ooo, yes! There's Oliver Owl. He's the magistrate. I'm sure he's a Proper Authority He looks ever so proper."

"So he does. And he gets more big official looking letters than anyone else in

Woodsey. Let's go and tell him about it."

So they went to see Oliver Owl and he was so interested that he came round right away. Magnus showed him where the chest was and Oliver stood looking down at it.

"How very interesting," he said at last. "You know, I do believe I know who buried that chest. Hoo yes. I'm sure I do."

"You do?" said Magnus, very excited.

"Hoo yes! Those initials—B.B.—I'm sure

I know whose they are—and after all, his shop did stand here, years ago, long before Woodsey Newtown was built. Bohuncus Bunny, his name was. He was a grocer."

"Bohuncus Bunny? Why—he was my Great-grandfather!" cried Bungle. "Of course—my old dad used to tell me about him. But I didn't know that this was where his shop used to be."

"Hoo, yes! I can just remember it," declared Oliver Owl. "I must have been a very young bird at the time—little more than an egg—but I well remember his funny old shop. And those are his initials—B.B.—so it is very likely that he buried this old chest. Of course, that would mean that the chest belongs to you, Bungle."

"To me?"

"Hoo, yes. Old Bohuncus buried it and now Magnus has found it again, you are the proper owner. Hoo, yes! Most legal! Hoo, yes indeed!"

Bungle was flabbergasted. "You mean that
if that chest is full of gold and jewels, they're
all mine?"

"Hoo, yes!"

"Well I never!" For the moment, Bungle
couldn't think of anything else to say, but
then he burst out, "Magnus found it, though.
So even if it is mine, he should have half of
it, shouldn't he? Then I'll give half to the
Woodsey orphanage and half to the old

folks' home and I'll keep the other half!"

"There'll only be two halves . . ." Oliver Owl pointed out.

"Oh—you know what I mean!" laughed Bungle, who was as excited as Magnus by now; so excited in fact that the two of them were dancing a little jig, round and round the old brass-bound chest.

"Of course," declared Oliver, as they skipped about, "we shall have to do this officially. Hoo, yes. Forms and things to fill in, you know. And we'll have to keep the chest at the Town Hall until everything is decided. Hoo, yes. That'll be a job for Scallywag-Fox. I'll send him round to collect the chest officially. Do him good to do some work for once. Hoo, yes!"

"I expect he'll be ever so pleased to hear the good news!" said Magnus, brightly.

But Scallywag-Fox wasn't a bit pleased. For one thing, he didn't like work and, for another, he sort of felt that since Magnus

wouldn't have found the chest if it hadn't
been for the cheese seeds, he, Jasper, ought to
have a share in the treasure.

"Most unfair, it is!" he told his crony,
Squeevey Squirrel. "But for me, that treasure
chest might have remained buried for ever!
And what thanks do I get? None! Just "run
round and collect the chest, and bring it to
the Town Hall, there's a good chap! Pah!"

"I think you've been treated very shabbily,
Jasper," agreed Squeevey solemnly, "and
how do they really know that the initials
stand for Bohuncus Bunny? They might
stand for Bosh Badger, or Billy Bison, or
Bertha Bear."

"How right you are!" declared Jasper.
"Or, they could be Bosco Bushtail. He was
my uncle, you know. Very weal——"

And Jasper stopped, as a great grin spread
over his crafty face. "Of course! Why didn't
I think of it before? I shall claim the chest
officially, as the property of my late Uncle

Bosco! I'll go round to Magnus Mouse's
house at once!"

And off dashed Jasper to fetch the treasure
chest in the official Town Hall wheel-barrow.
He told Magnus nothing about his scheme to
claim the treasure chest and tore back to the
Town Hall with it, where Mayor Mole locked
it up in the official town hall strong room.

When the door was locked, Jasper cleared
his throat importantly.

"A-hem! Please, Mr Mayor, I wish to make an official claim to the treasure chest."

"You do?" Mayor Mole wasn't really all that surprised; Jasper Scallywag-Fox was always trying some scheme to get rich quickly. "And what makes you think it might be yours?"

"The initials on the lid, Mr Mayor. They are the initials of my late uncle, Bosco Bushtail. I think that chest contains his fortune, which ought to be mine, by rights."

"Well—if that is the case, then you certainly have a claim. Go and see Mr Owl, and he will take all the particulars. By the way, I can't find my bottle of red ink anywhere. I suppose you haven't seen it, have you?"

"Er—eh—wassat? Red ink?" Jasper went very red himself. "Er—no—I haven't got it—I mean seen it. I must hurry and catch Mr Owl now, please Mr Mayor . . ."

And Jasper dashed off.

"I wonder why he wanted a bottle of red ink, now?" Mr Mole wondered to himself.

Jasper went straight round to Oliver Owl's house and told him all about his Uncle Bosco. Oliver, who knew well what a rogue Jasper was, couldn't help thinking that Jasper was trying it on. But he had to be fair to him and, as a matter of fact, he had known Jasper's Uncle Bosco quite well. So even though he felt sure that B.B. stood for Bohuncus Bunny, he had to let Jasper make his claim.

"Hoooo!" he said, when Jasper had finished telling his tale, "have to get that all down officially, you know. Hoo, yes! Now—I think I have the right form here. Would you kindly fill it in, please?"

And he produced the biggest yellow form you've ever seen from his desk.

"Fill it all in, Mr Fox. Put down all the details. Mustn't miss anything out. Hoo, no!"

Mr Owl almost felt sorry for Jasper at that moment. The form was really about permission to dig a new drain, but Jasper didn't know that, and he worked away, putting down all the bits about the colour of his eyes and his grandmother's maiden name and the address of the premises hereinunder and all sorts of things that you put on forms.

When he'd done, Oliver Owl took the form from him, bonked it with a rubber stamp and put it away in his desk.

"We'll soon settle the problem now," he declared. "Hoo, yes! As soon as we get that chest open, I'm sure we shall find something inside to tell us the true owner. Hoo, yes! We'll get Wilf Weasel to open it tomorrow,

at the Town Hall. You'll want to be there,
no doubt? You mustn't miss that. Hoo, no!"

Meanwhile, Magnus Mouse had gone
back to his gardening and Bungle Bunny
had gone home to tell his wife, Bingle, about
the treasure chest. Magnus was just digging
a row of neat little holes, to plant his precious
cheese seeds, when his wife Martha called to
him from the back door.

"Magnus—shall we have those millet seeds

for supper?"

"Millet seeds?" replied Magnus frowning. "Yes, of course. But what millet seeds?"

"The ones you put in the sideboard. You are a one, labelling them cheese seeds. I've washed that red stuff off them and they're delicious. They'll make a lovely supper."

"B-b-bbut they are cheese seeds!" cried Magnus, letting the secret out without meaning to.

"Silly Magnus!" said Martha. "Anybody knows there's no such thing. You make cheese from milk, not seeds. Who told you they were cheese seeds?"

"Mr Fox," said Magnus, suddenly feeling rather foolish.

"Hmph! Him!" snorted Martha. "What does he know about it? He couldn't tell a seed from a suet dumpling."

And Martha slammed the door as she went back into the house to cook the millet supper.

Magnus looked terribly crestfallen. Even

then, he didn't really think Jasper had
swindled him.

"He must have made a mistake," he
decided. "I'll tell him, when I see him."

The next day they all gathered at the
Town Hall for the official opening of the

treasure chest. Oliver Owl and Mayor Mole were in charge and Wilf Weasel was there with all the things he'd need.

While they were waiting to start, Magnus spoke to Jasper. "Please, Mr Fox," he said, "you made a mistake. Those weren't cheese seeds at all. They were millet. Would you please give me my five pounds back?"

Jasper nearly had a fit! He went bright scarlet and nearly choked! But, much to his relief, Mr Owl called the meeting to order just then and Magnus couldn't ask him any more awkward questions!

"Hooo! Quiet please!" said Mr Owl. "We are here to open the treasure chest, which Magnus Mouse found in his garden, and to decide whether it was buried there by Bohuncus Bunny, or Bosco Bushtail and whether it is now the property of Bungle Bunny, or Jasper Scallywag-Fox. Hoo, yes!"

Magnus gave Jasper rather a surprised look on hearing this, but Oliver Owl went on:

"Open the chest, Mr Weasel!"

Wilf Weasel, who kept the Woodsey garage, and was a very clever inventor, opened his big tool box, and took out a pair of very strong cutters. They were rather like a pair of big shears, with short blades and very long handles. You could have heard a pin drop as he went to work.

Chonk! Chonk!

First one padlock was cut and then the

other. Wilf pulled the padlocks away and then pulled up the lid. The chest opened with a loud creak.

They all crowded round.

The inside of the chest was completely filled with a large package, tightly wrapped in old-fashioned oilskin—the sort of thing that waterproof coats were once made of—and on top of this mysterious parcel was a folded sheet of paper, yellow with age, and sealed with a big red wax seal.

"Aha!" said Oliver Owl. "A legal document, if I am not mistaken! Now we shall learn the truth! Hoo, yes!"

Oliver Owl broke the seal and unfolded the paper. Everybody held their breath, as he began to read.

It sounded ever so important.

"Know ye one and all, whosoever," read Mr Owl, "that this is written by me. Packed in this chest is something of great value, which will become more valuable as the years

pass by. I have been keeping it and feasting
my eyes upon it for many years now and I
now bury it under the ground, so that those
who come after me may enjoy it when it is
found." Mr Owl paused, and looked up. "It
is signed 'Bohuncus Bunny'," he ended.

"It really is yours, Bungle! I am pleased!"
cried Magnus Mouse, while Jasper ground
his teeth in disappointment.

"Oh goody!" breathed Bungle. "I am

lucky! I'll share it with just everybody! But what is it?"

"I suggest you unwrap the oilskin and find out!" said Mr Owl.

His fingers trembling with excitement, Bungle Bunny untied the tapes, which held the big parcel together and then began to peel off the oilskin, which had gone a bit gummy and was stuck to itself all over.

The parcel was sort of barrel shaped, and quite heavy, as Bungle discovered when he heaved it out of the chest.

"Whatever can it be?" he wondered.

"Perhaps it's a keg of golden sovereigns!" breathed Magnus.

Even Scallywag-Fox had forgotten his great disappointment for the moment, and was watching eagerly, as the oilskin came off, layer after layer and mostly in little bits, for it had become very brittle with age.

At last Bungle Bunny pulled away the final layer of wrapping from the mysterious

shape and there, before their eyes, was a
huge and ancient Stilton Cheese!

"Pher-yew!" cried Bungle Bunny
staggering back and almost all the others
jumped hurriedly away as well. After all
those years, it really was the ripest ripe
Stilton Cheese you could possibly imagine!

But Magnus Mouse didn't jump back. He
just stood there, with a rapturous expression
on his face, breathing in what seemed to him

the most wonderful smell he had ever smelled!

"How blissy!" he cried. "What a yummy smell! The cheeseyest cheese of all! What could be cheeseyer than a genuine antique Stilton! I just know it will taste yummy!"

Well, of course, he was quite right. Any real cheese expert will tell you that the worse a cheese smells, the better it tastes. And this one smelled terrible!

Terrible! At least, that's what everyone but Magnus thought. To him it smelled so heavenly, that it quite made up for not having a cheese garden.

Bungle Bunny kept his promise to share the treasure cheese with everyone and that following Saturday, they had the great Woodsey Newtown Treasure Cheese Party.

Just everyone was there and everyone agreed that the cheese tasted as good as it smelled bad.

Of course, they had to hold the party out of doors . . .